YOU'RE MARRIED DON'T ACT SINGLE.

YOU'RE SINGLE DON'T PLAY MARRIED.

Desree Scott

authorHOUSE®

AuthorHouse™ LLC
1663 Liberty Drive
Bloomington, IN 47403
www.authorhouse.com
Phone: 1-800-839-8640

Published by AuthorHouse 06/06/2014

ISBN: 978-1-4969-1828-4 (sc)
ISBN: 978-1-4969-1827-7 (e)

CONTENTS

CHAPTER 1

Nikkie and Stacie was out at the mall shopping and enjoying their two weeks vacation trying to decide if they were going anywhere.

"So lady, are you still seeing Willie?" Stacie asked Nikkie.

"Yes I am and don't start! I know he is a married man, but we love each other and soon he will be leaving his wife. He told me so," said Nikkie as a good-looking young man walked up.

"Hello ladies," He said. "Do you need any help?"

"No." said Stacie.

"Yes, I do." said Nikkie. "How would I go about getting your number?"

"Well I am married," said the young man.

"So?" Nikkie said and handed him a pen and paper. He wrote on it, handed it back, and then walked away.

"Bastard." Nikkie said. No one heard her but Stacie.

"What? Let me see. Stacie looked at the paper and it said *I am married.* Stacie laughed as Nikkie walked away to go to the check out lane.

"You find that funny?" asked Nikkie.

"Why are you so stuck on married men anyway? If they cheat on their wife with another female what do they think about that female they're cheating with?" asked Stacie.

"Look, I don't care. A married man to me is money because if you find the married man that wants to sneak but don't want to mess up his home he will pay a person like me to keep my mouth shut. I get

1

400.00 a week from Willie. Plus he pays my bills and that nice car I drive in. That's his wife's money so see I just don't mess around with married men, I mess with stupid married men." said NIKKIE as she paid for her items and walked out to get in her car. As the two got in the car Willie pulled up and got out and walked in the store hugging and kissing all over his wife. Nikkie noticed him and said, "Look at that! I will be calling him. I should go confront him but I don't want to mess up my money." So she drove off.

"Get what you want." Willie told his wife. "This is your day. Baby I love you so." Willie found a seat and sat down while his wife Joyce shopped and got what she wanted.

Cathy and Darryl walked out the movies laughing and holding on to each other. "So baby," said Cathy as the two got into the car. "You want to grab a bite to eat?"

"Yes," said Darryl. "Honey I got one thing to do and I will fly home to pick you up so we can get that bite." Cathy looked over at her husband and said,

"Do you love me? Am I enough for you?"

"What? said Darryl. "Baby yes I love you, and you are more than enough woman for me. I need you in every way and don't you forget that." CATHY looked over at him and said,

"You better mean ever word of that Mr."

Over at Christy and James' house Christy was saying, "I want you out of my life! I hate you James! You are a liar and a cheat! Get out!" As Christy started throwing his things out she yelled, "Get out!" James grabbed her.

"Wait, please lets talk. I love you and I am sorry, very sorry. Give me one chance to make this right. Please hear me out, you're my wife and I will do what I have to do to get you back." Christy pushed James away from her.

"You got nerves to stand here and ask for forgiveness after you cheated and gave me H.I.V! Get out please get out. James Kissed her and said before walking out,

"I won't give up on us."

Nikkie and Darryl sat at the coffee shop drinking coffee and eating donuts. "So are we still going to Florida?" Nikkie asked Darryl. "Because I had fun in Washington. "It was me and you and no one to hide from." As Darryl reached for Nikkie's hand he said,

"No I cant, my wife-"

"Wait a minute." said Nikkie. "Who is your wife? She wasn't your wife last night or the night before. So Darryl please don't give me that wife shit. Are we going to Florida?" Darryl let go of her hand and said,

"Like I was saying me and my wife Cathy are going to Florida. Look I love my wife and you are not the woman I would want to bear my kids or carry my last name. As of this day you and me are over. Don't call me, text me, or email me. I am finished with you." He stood up and walked away.

"Wait." said Nikkie. "You think you call the shots after three years? Baby it won't be that easy."

"Stay away." Darryl said. He left her standing there with tears in her eyes on his way to eat with his wife. Suddenly her phone rang as she started towards her car.

"Hello?"

"What's up?" Willie said on the other end.

"You must be done playing the good husband. I saw you today acting like you love her. Nikkie said.

"Whatever. Lets get together. I haven't seen you in two weeks."

"Fine," said Nikkie. "I will call you later."

"Bet." said Willie and hung up.

CHAPTER 2

James and his best friend David were at the gym working out man. "What's up?" David asked James. "You done had a long face since we been in here."

"Christy put me out and it hurts. Man I miss my wife. I love her, and I messed up, but we can fix this. I haven't touched my wife over a year now because after I did what I done that part of our lives went out the window. I feel in my heart we can work this out if she gives us one more chance."

"Look," said David. Okay you gave her H.I.V. so it really doesn't matter if you two sleep together or not. Yes she is mad at you but dude you been hanging in trying to get it right with you two just leave and call it off. I would. James looked at David and laughed.

"Leave? Just like that? I don't know why I am talking to a man that don't even have a woman or a wife.

Stacie and Shell was hanging out at the park walking and having girl talk. "Have you seen Nikkie?" Shell asked Stacie.

"Yes I have. We was at the mall the other day together."

" I haven't seen her in a week." said Shell. "So how is she?"

"Fine. Said Stacie. "I just get so worried about her dealing with these married men. Nothing good will come out of sleeping with a man who is married or just sleeping around when you're not married. I ask Nikkie to go to church to pray and ask God to send her a husband and believe He will. It won't be on her time, it will be on his. Patience is a must."

"Well, said Shell. "I pray for her day and night."

As Cathy and Darryl enjoyed their outing together the two went into the house. Cathy went to the bedroom and began to undress so she could take a shower. Darryl went in the room and tried helping her, "Stop." she said. "Not tonight. I'm not up to this. Maybe in two weeks. I love you." Then she went and got into the shower.

"What?" Darryl got in the shower with her with all his cloths on. "Two weeks? You are my wife. Every time I want to make love to my wife I got to go through this? So you put me on a schedule? I give you anything you ask for. I make sure you need nothing. I bend over backwards for you but I cant make love to my wife? I need you Cathy!" Darryl tried kissing her on her neck but she pushed him away.

"Stop, please! Let me take my shower!"

"Fine." said Darryl as he got out.

CHAPTER 3

Christy was visiting her doctor and he was saying, "Have you been taking you medicine?" Yes both me and my husband have."

"Well Christy tell him I won't be sending him any more pills. Even though you said you got H.I.V from him he needs to be checked as well. It has been a year and I have not seen him one time and his condition could be worse than yours."

"Okay." said Christy. "We're supposed to meet for dinner tonight and I will tell him. After all this I can't stand the sight of my own husband. I am his wife but he cheated and this is what he brings me home."

Shell and Stacie were having dinner when Nikkie and Willie walked in and went over to their table. "Hi ladies." Nikkie said. "You got room for two more?"

"Sure." said shell. "Sit down. What you been up to?" They sat down and Willie put his arm around Nikkie.

"I don't want to be rude or make anyone feel uncomfortable," said Stacie. "But Mr. Willie how can you sleep at night knowing that you're sleeping around on your wife? All the things you do are not pleasing in God's eyes." Nikkie interrupted.

"Please don't start. We love each other."

"Love?" said Stacie. "Are you serious?" He cheats on his wife and you would rather burn in hell for this man? If this is how he treats the woman he's married to how do you think he will treat you? Look I don't want to sit here and watch you look like a fool. I am leaving."

"Wait!" Shell said as she gathered her things. "I am leaving with you."

"Oh." Nikkie said. "It's like this?"

"Are you coming to church Sunday?" Asked Shell.

"No." Said Nikkie. "Me and Willie have family time this Sunday." Stacie laughed and both females walked away. Willie kissed Nikkie and said,

"I love you. Both of them are jealous of you. To me you are my wife.

CHAPTER 4

Christy and James sat at the coffee house. She ordered iced tea and he had coffee with cream and no sugar. "Look." said James. "Baby I understand that I made a bad mistake but I am trying to get things right with you and me. I love you. I need you in my life. Work with me please. I slept with another woman, yes I did. It was over a year ago but yet I am still here trying to get my wife back. This has been a long year for me. You gave me the do"s and don't and I done nothing but what you ask of me. I would love to make love to you again but you said this would be a marriage without sex. I am fine with that cause I love you and will do what it takes to show you. But help me please take one step. Let me come back home. Please."

"No." said Christy. "I can't. Not at this moment. You hurt me. You let another woman in our life; and not only that, you gave me H.I.V. My marriage was everything. I would have never done this to you."

"Ok." Said James. Baby Sunday when we go to church lets go to the pastor and ask for prayer together. Maybe we can't change what has happened but God can change our situation."

"No. You need prayer, not me. I will be filing for divorce. I don't want you anymore ."James began to cry and beg.

"Christy, please! On my life I won't hurt you again! Whatever it takes I will do it. Just say it please."

"I want you to leave me alone." Christy said. "You done your do but you got H.I.V and you're afraid another woman won't want you. You want to make us work because you feel I am your only choice. You and me are over." James held her hand and said,

"I won't stop trying. I put all this in God's hands and I know His will shall be done.

CHAPTER 5

Darryl was at his office finishing up a few papers before his vacation and his phone rang. "Hello, Darryl Manns."

"Hi honey." said Nikkie. "I Got your page last night. What's up?"

"Look I shouldn't have called you." I'm trying to do right by my wife but at times I think about you. I'm sorry for calling."

"Look," said Nikki. "Your wife could never be me and I am the one who makes you happy. So I will be at the Rico Hotel. Come by and see me." She hung up. Willie went home to see his wife, Joyce, going over the account.

"Willie." She said. "You took five hundred dollars out the account. What was it used for?" He hung up his coat. "It was a personal matter. I took care of a few things." Said Willie.

"Personal Matter?" Said Joyce. "I would like to know what it was for." Willie sat next to his wife.

"Look, that's my money. I do what I want with it."

"Willie," Joyce said in a soft voice. "I am your wife and I have the right to know what you needed money like that for. We never made decisions about money alone. We've always done that together. You need to tell me something." Willie stood up and smacked Joyce across her face. "You never ask me about money I make! You never had to ask for nothing!" Then he walked away. Joyce held her face while she cried and whispered,

"What is wrong with you?"

CHAPTER 6

Pastor Williams sat in his office waiting on his next appointment. A knock came at the door. "Come in." said Pastor. "Hi." Said Darryl.

"Hello. Said Pastor. "Have a seat. How are you? Is your wife Cathy coming today?"

"No." said Darryl. "I needed to talk to you alone. I have sinned against my wife more than once and every time I try to do right I do wrong. Cathy hasn't had sex with me in weeks and I feel I am not the man she wants anymore. So I do what I do to feel loved."

"Darryl." Said the pastor. Do you hear yourself? It seems to me you're finding reason to make yourself feel better on why you do what you really want to do. No matter what you and your wife goes through cheating is not the answer. You are supposed to love your wife like Christ loves his church. If you try talking to her about it and it don't work take it to God over and over."

"But this is not a way to fix things. What must I do? I feel bad that I've done this. Help me pastor." Said Darryl.

"Pray." Said pastor. "Ask for forgiveness and never do this again. Repent to the Lord and ask him to work on whatever is bothering your wife."

"Pray? I don't know how."

"Take my hand." Said pastor as the two stood up. "Tell God how you feel. Ask Him whatever you want to know and believe that the Lord will work in your life." Darryl began to pray.

"Help me Lord to do what's right. I am sorry for what I've done. Show me how to be a better husband. Help my wife with what ever she is going through. I need you Lord. Forgive me please." Pastor said,

"Do you believe that the Lord will work in your life? Do you believe you can be that good husband? Are you willing to let go and let God?"

"Yes." Pastor hugged him and said,

"All you got to do is have faith and watch what the lord can do."

Stacie was in the shoe store looking for a black pair of dress shoes when a woman walked up and said, "That is a nice pair. I like them. I need a black pair myself. By the way my name is Christy."

"Good to meet you. I am Stacie." The two shook hands.

"So," said Christy. "You got a hot date?"

"No." Stacie said. "I am single. The only man in my life is Jesus and I am very happy. So do you have a hot date?"

"No I don't. I am shopping to let off steam. My husband and me are not on good terms at this time."

Joyce was at her mother's house, miss Murphy, telling her what happened with her and Willie. "Look baby," said her mom. "You aren't any one's fool and you and all married women need to check accounts. If a man can't tell you penny for penny then something is not right. Either he's on drugs, gambling, or taking care of someone you don't know about."

"Mama," said Joyce. "Maybe he is in debt and don't want me to know."

"Okay child. If that is what you want to think, but you need to investigate. See we as woman are very smart. We sense when something is not right and our sense that the good Lord gave us honey don't lie."

"I just pray mama."

"Okay baby that's fine. Pray because the lord can work this out for you, but he wants you to use your sense as well. But go ahead and act like a fool if you want and God will be there because he takes care of fools and babies."

"Mama I don't know what to say to him. He said his money is his business."

"When he married you his business became your business and when you go to church tomorrow pray for the lord to let you see things. " Said Miss Murphy. "Just don't get upset when he shows you."

CHAPTER 7

Cathy was at home fixing up the table to surprise her husband Darryl with a candle light dinner and a little fun afterwards. She kept trying to reach him on his cell but there was no answer so she decided to leave a message. "Hi honey its your wife. Sorry for how I've been acting. I love you and need you in my life. Call me or I will see you when you get home. Bye."

Sunday morning Willie and Joyce was finishing up getting ready for church and Willie said, "Look Joyce, I am sorry for how I acted and I should have never put my hands on you. But I still mean what I said. My money is my business." Joyce grabbed her jacket to go out the door.

"Look Willie you got it wrong. Your money is my business and I looked at the account again and you've got five hundred coming out ever week. You will tell me why one day. I trust the Lord on that. She left and slammed the door. Willie grabbed his coat and left so the two could make it to church.

As Stacie and Shell walked in church, Christy was waving for them to come and sit next to her. "Who is that?" Asked James.

"I met her in the store." as Stacie walked up to say hi the two hugged. "Christy," Stacie said. "This is my friend Shell, and everyone this is Christy." Everyone said hi and sat down. Cathy walked in and had a seat then David walked in behind her and sat down as the choir began to sing "cant no body do me like Jesus".

Darryl sat up on the bed and look over at Nikkie. As she lay there with nothing but a sheet covering her. She rolled over. "Darryl baby what's wrong?" she asked him.

"Nothing." He said as he got up to get dressed.

"Look," said Nikkie. "Last night was great, but I heard you when you said you can't do this anymore. Okay, fine. But I want my money."

"Money? You can have this five hundred." He tossed it at her. "We are done."

"So you think. You will give me this every week like you've been doing for the past two years. When my money stop I will tell miss Cathy everything."

"What? You stupid-" Darryl caught himself and headed to the door. Then he turned and said, "Okay Nikkie. You will get your money."

"Children of God," said the pastor. "The Lord has put a word on my heart and I got a message for someone in here today. Turn your bibles to Philippians 4:19. Let us read together. *But my God shall supply all your needs according to his riches in glory by Christ Jesus amen.*" As the pastor began preaching Cathy cried knowing that her marriage was on the rocks. However, she was also praising God because she knew that no matter what the Lord would help her through this tough time in her life.

As Darryl walked through the door he noticed that the table was set for a candle light dinner. He sat at the table and put his head down in shame yelling, dear Lord! What have I done? Help me! Please help me!" A knock came at the door. "Who is it?" He went to the door.

"Well it is your favorite mother-in-law boy open this door," said Miss Hunter. Darryl opened the door and walked away.

"Your daughter is not here." he said. Miss Hunter closed the door behind her.

"I know that. I am sure my daughter is at church asking the Lord to help her deal with you."

"What do you want?" Darryl said in a rude voice.

"No what do you want?" Miss Hunter said as she sat down. "Look my daughter tells me everything and I never get involved in your marriage but a husband don't stay gone from home all-night to sleep with another woman-"

"Look you don't know a damn thing so please get the hell out my house." Miss Hunter stood up and said,

"Okay. I will leave because this is your house, but baby I didn't make sixty-one being dumb. I know when a man is cheating. I had one. I didn't come to kick you while you are down. I came to pray with you and ask the Lord to forgive you. I was hoping you and my daughter could make it through this. For God has a blessing in store. But you got to get this right. To get it we all make mistakes but change is good for us. You're hurting your wife and there's nothing worse then an angry God." Miss Hunter left and Darryl just stood there.

As everyone was leaving the church pastor asked James and Christy to see him in his office. "Come in and sit down." Said the pastor. "I need to talk to you two." Before he could get a word out Christy began to speak in a rude and upset way.

"Look I don't want this man anymore. I don't love him or need him. He has destroyed our marriage and my life. How can you forgive a person who has cheated over and over and given you H.I.V and acts like nothing has happened? I hate this man I married!" said Christy.

"Wait baby," Said James. "I am sorry. What do you want me to do? I will do it. I will say what you want me to say. I love you and God knows I am sorry. Please don't walk away. I need you. I love you. I am sorry! Pastor please tell me what I can do to get my wife back. Help me! James started crying but Christy not once looked at her husband. She blurted,

"Honey save the tears."

"Christy, said the pastor. "I know you are hurting and upset but healing comes with forgiving." Christy jumped up and said,

"Well I will never heal," and walked out.

"Look James, that is your wife. For everything that we do there is a consequence. You keep looking to God. Pray for Christy because you two can get through this together. No matter what continue to love her.

CHAPTER 8

Cathy walked in the house to see Darryl sitting on the couch watching TV. She sat next to him. "Darryl, look honey-"

"Don't start okay? Last night I stayed with a buddy of mine and I don't feel like your mess today." Cathy stood up and said,

"Okay Darryl, that's fine. That's not a problem." She went into the bedroom and Darryl sat there for a minute before he began to hear a lot of things being moved around. He got up to go into the bedroom to see what was going on and saw Cathy packing.

"What the hell are you doing?" he asked her.

"I am leaving. I want a divorce. I can't do this anymore."

"A divorce?" said Darryl. "Okay you can get that but before you leave give me back everything I bought you starting with that outfit you got on."

"What?" said Cathy.

"You heard me. Give me my things." Darryl went up to Cathy and he began to rip the cloths off her. She was screaming,

"Stop! Please stop! Don't do this!"

"You leaving?" Darryl asked. "You want to leave right?"

CHAPTER 9

Stacie, Nikkie, and Shell were out having dinner. "So Nikkie," Said Shell. "It has been a while since we seen you. What you been up to?"

"Not much." Nikkie said. "Just tired of the same old stuff. I want to do something different. This life I am living don't feel right anymore. I used to enjoy it but for the first time I feel like this life is really wrong."

"Well," Said Stacie. "Dealing with men who are not yours will leave you in a bad satiation."

"Look," said Nikkie. "Cant' you just listen and stop preaching all the time? Every time I say something you want to preach. I know where a lot of churches are."

"So go." Said Shell. "Look we care about you and want you to do what is right. Sleeping with married men is not right. Nothing good will come from that."

"Well," said Nikkie. "Dealing with married men can pay off. I get five hundred dollars a week from both married men and I call it hush money. See they're sinning not me. I'm not married." Stacie laughed.

"Are you serious? You believe that you're right for doing what you do? Black mailing married men? You are a top sales person at the real estate. You own your own home, five cars, no kids very pretty. They care nothing for you. They don't even care for their wives. They are dogs."

"That's cool." said Nikkie. "I am a female dog." Shell handed Nikkie a small bible and said,

"In your spare time read John 1:9." Nikkie glanced at the verse quickly and read it out loud. *If we confess our sins-* Then she put it in her purse.

"Okay," she said. I will read it. I promise.

CHAPTER 10

Joyce and Willie were at the table eating dinner. "How was your day?" asked Joyce.

"It could have been better." said Willie. "But tomorrow I will be home late so there's no need to wait up for me."

"Okay You've been coming home late almost every night. Are you cheating on me?" Willie got up and walked over to her. He kissed Joyce on her forehead.

"Don't start. I am going to bed."

James was at David's house watching a late game on TV. "Want a beer?" asked David.

"No," James said. "I want my wife back."

"Look man she is not coming back. Move on. Let it go. Maybe she has someone else."

"Someone like who?" Asked James.

"I don't know but it is your woman who has H.I.V.you mean my wife. She loves me and never cheated on me."

"I messed up not her." said James. "I don't know what to do or say. I've been begging hard and I won't stop. She said I can come and see her Friday. She has something to talk to me about and I got a feeling she is going to give me one more chance."

"James man tell her you want a divorce and watch how quick she takes you back. See you beg too much. We got to play hard sometimes and women change quick. Act like you don't care."

"That's my wife." Said James. "Playing hard won't get her back. I see why you single." David laughed.

"I do have someone and you will see her one day. Just right at this moment a lot is going on. But you will meet her soon very soon.

CHAPTER 11

A knock came at Miss Hunter's door. "Hi mama." Said Cindy with bags in her hand and a big smile. She hugged her mama and walked in with Ronald behind her.

"You two come in and have a seat," Said mama Hunter. "Are you hungry? Want some tea?"

"No thanks," Cindy said as the two placed their bags down.

"So how long are you staying?"

"A week at the most," said Ronald as he gave his mother-in-law a hug. "I got a lot to do at work and business is good."

"I wanted to come and see you mama and check on my baby sister," Cindy said. "How is she doing?"

"Go ask her," said Miss Hunter. "She is in the guestroom. While you going to see about your sister I want my son in-law to take me for a ride in that brand new hummer he got you."

"Lets go mama," said Ronald. Cindy walked in the room to see Cathy looking out the window.

"Sis are you ok?" Cindy asked. Cathy turned around and both eyes were black, she had a busted lip, and one side of her face was swollen. "Oh my God!" Cindy said and hugged her sister. "Who did this to you? Cathy tell me what happened!" The two sat on the bed holding hands.

"I can't do this anymore sis," said Cathy. "Me and Darryl have became strangers in our marriage. I promise I don't know him anymore. He stays away from home maybe a week at a time. He's drinking daily and money is missing from his account and I don't know where it is going. He keeps lying and I believe he has another woman. I can feel it in my heart. Now look; this is what my husband has done to me. I told him I was leaving but before I could go he ripped off my cloths, raped, and beat me! Can you believe that my husband of ten years could do this? No man should treat his wife like she is trash. I am too afraid to go back. I am scared of him, but I love him the same as I did when I married him. Do you think I'm stupid?"

"No," said Cindy. "He is your husband and you got that right to still love him. Mama always said you were the strong one. You got a good forgiving heart and you take so much and that don't mean a person is stupid. To me it means a person is just stronger than me. See God don't put more on us than we can bear and he knew you were going to have a crazy man. So trust me he gave you strength to deal with it and its ok to be scared of your husband. God will see you through."

"I don't know what to do or say."

"Cathy give me your hand and let's pray. Dear God, one of your children is hurting and she doesn't understand why. Lord she needs healing right now. Her road is very rocky and any decisions she makes father she needs you to be in the mist. For we know you sit high and look low and there is nothing you can't do. You said ask in your name and it shall be done so we ask you father for help. I am pleading for my sister and Darryl that both of them put all trust in you amen."

"Thank you," said Cathy. "I love you sis."

CHAPTER 12

"Okay ladies," said Doctor Anderson. "Let it out. Classes will be starting in one minute so grab your refreshments. Welcome first time visitors. Take your seats and we will start from left to right introducing ourselves."

"Hi my name is Joyce."

"Hi my name is Christy and I brought two friends of my Stacie and Shell. Stacie and me met at the shoe store a while back and we've gotten close. I told them about these classes I attend and both wanted to come and support me."

"That's great," said Doctor Anderson. "Welcome. Okay and your name."

"Hi my name is Ruby."

"My name is Debbie."

"Okay ladies let's get started. Last week we talked about time for ourselves and sometimes being married we forget ourselves. Everyone else is first and when the day is done from cooking, cleaning, and working we find ourselves over whelmed and tired. After so long of doing this it may lead to depression. Women are everything to everybody and we need time to be able to unwind by reading a book, taking a walk, getting with friends, or watching a movie. I told everyone to try to take time for herself." Ruby raised her hand.

"I went to the library and read a couple of books. I had a light lunch alone and walked in the park."

"How did you feel afterwards?" asked the Doctor.

"Great. It gave me peace of mind." said Ruby. "My husband works and I don't so he calls me over fifty times while he's working. I usually stay home to do what needs to be done at home. I don't go anywhere until he gets home and even then he is the one who will take me for a ride. I felt locked up and stressed but after I came home from a day to myself I felt ready to do what needed to be done. I was able to regroup and it felt so good that I decided to take a day for myself once a week." Everyone clapped for her.

"Anyone else?" said the doctor. Christy raised her hand.

"I went out for the first time in awhile with Stacie and Shell. We went to the coffee house then went and got our nails done and to see a movie. It was a very peaceful day."

"Good," said Doctor Anderson. "Ladies you won't believe what a few hours away for yourself can do. The difference it will make to yourself and the ones who live with you its amazing.

CHAPTER 13

Darryl got out of bed and went downstairs to see Nikkie cooking him breakfast. "Hi honey." She kissed him as he sat at the table and she placed his food in front of him.

"Baby," said Darryl as Nikkie sat down to eat with him. "I wish my wife was like you."

"Are you serious?" said Nikkie as she smiled. "What she don't cook you breakfast?"

"Yes," said Darryl. "She cooks but you are a fool. You do anything I ask. You fool with me knowing you could never have me. You have no self-respect for yourself and I can talk to you any way I want. You're not in my business. You like a dummy that I control. You speak when told. I always wanted a street woman with no morals or respect but I'm good because I got you. Oh and by the way the pancakes are good."

James was driving after picking up his wife some flowers and was heading to go see her. An oncoming, speeding car that was running from the police lost control of his car hit James head on.

Willie and Joyce got into the car after having dinner. "I know I haven't been the best husband and I've done a lot of things wrong but baby I am tired. I am so tired. My heart is heavy and my nights are like days. I can't sleep. I got to talk to you and I want to tell you the truth but I'm scared. Will the truth run you away or will you give me a chance to make it right?" asked Willie.

"Tell me the truth," said Joyce. "I am your wife. I love you and I won't run. I may cry but I won't run."

Miss Hunter and Ronald made it back from the thrifty store where she loves to shop. Cindy and Cathy were in the dinning room laughing and talking. As Ronald walked in the dinning room he said, "Stop all that noise you two. How are you doing Cathy?"

"I am better. My face is healing."

"She is going to be just fine," said Cindy.

"Yes my baby is." said their mother as she walked in the room. She is a child of God and he will take care of Cathy. I believe that and I know that.

CHAPTER 14

Christy was at home signing her divorce papers and her phone rang. "Hello?"

"May I speak to Christy Jones?"

"This is here."

"Hello, I am the nurse at Wealth Hospital and your husband James Jones was in a car accident and was brought here an hour ago."

"Thank you," said Christy. "I will be right there." she hung up and called David.

Darryl was on his couch at home sleep and a knock came at his door. "Who is it and what do you want?" yelled Darryl.

"Open the door," said Ronald. As the door open Ronald walked in.

"What up bro?" said Darryl as he closed the door. "When you get in town ?"

"Lord forgive me for what I am about to do to this man," said Ronald. He hit Darryl so hard that he went over the couch and he hit him again and again till Darryl began to beg for his life.

"Stop please! Stop you going to kill me man! I am sorry for what I've done to your wife's sister! I am sorry for what I've done to Cathy! Please stop!" Ronald helped Darryl off the floor.

"What is wrong with you man? You beat your wife like that! It was wrong! What happened to you loving her?"

CHAPTER 15

As Willie and Joyce laid in the bed, Willie began to talk to his wife. "I married you Joyce because you were the woman I fell in love with. I wanted you to be the mother of my kids. You're strong, kind, have a heart of gold, sexy, and most of all you believe in Jesus. When I stopped praying you prayed for me and I know you've been praying for me because I am still here. I wasn't praying for you or myself and I thank you for not giving up on me. I want to get it right with you and me and I promise I will tell you everything just ask me. There will be no more lying." Joyce sat up and looked at her husband and said,

"So I can ask where you been all these nights and if you're having an affair and you will answer with the truth?"

"Yes I will," said Willie. "No more lies. My focus is to make you love and trust me like you once did."

"Look," said Joyce. "I love you and I don't want to take you through pain for telling me anything. All I want you to do is stop it all tomorrow. Take that day and handle what you need to do because I don't want our marriage this way. If you are willing to try I am willing to try as well. Me and you." Willie kissed her and said,

"Yes. Me and you."

Over at the hospital Christy and David sit in the waiting room. "It will be ok," said David. "James is a strong man. He will pull through this."

"I feel numb," said Christy. "I got so much hate towards this man, my husband, who has done so much to me. I brought the divorce papers for him to sign because me and him are finished."

"Do you want to give them to him now?" asked David.

"Yes. The sooner the better."

"Do you have two copies?"

"Yes. Would you like to see one?" As Christy handed David a copy to read Doctor Steven walked into the room and said,

"Hi. You must be James' wife. Mrs. Jones?"

"Yes I am. When can I see him because he has to sign these divorce papers."

"Well," Doctor Steven said. "I am sorry but your husband can't sign anything today because he is in a coma."

Stacie and Shell were at Nikkie's house enjoying the day together. "Guess what Darryl called me the other day," Nikkie said. "He called me Mary."

"See girl you need to read your bible a little more." said Shell. "Mary Magdalene is a prostitute in the bible. Jesus cast seven devils out of her so that goes to show how he thinks of you."

"Look," said Stacie. "When are you going to stop dealing with these married men? Nikkie you're getting nothing out of this but pain in the long run. I don't care how much hush money they pay you. All money is not good money."

"Are you two done?" asked Nikkie. "Nothing good comes from being faithful either. I was with Carl for nine long years and he cheated every time I changed my clothes. I was a good wife to him and he married the one he cheated with on me so maybe Darryl will leave his wife and marry me."

"Maybe Carl wasn't for you," said Shell. "I am sure Darryl is not the man for you either and if he's not a man sent by God you don't wont him anyway."

"How will I know if he is a man sent by God?"

"First you need to get to know Jesus by reading his word, going to church to praise and worship him, and letting him in your life. The closer you get to Jesus things will start happening in your life and the old you will become a new you. Then when a good man is sent by Jesus you will know." said shell.

Christy walked in to the room to see James hooked up to many different monitors. "James can you hear me?" she said as a tear came from her eye. "It's been three weeks and I need to talk to you so please wake up." Then she walked out the room.

Cathy went to the construction company that her husband owns and Darryl noticed her walking across the field. As the two got closer Darryl said, "I knew it wouldn't be long for you to realize I am the man. You are more than welcome to come home and yes I forgive you."

"No." said Cathy. "I am here because the mail carrier takes too long. I wanted to bring these papers as fast as I could. Oh and Darryl, I forgive you." she walked away. When he opened the envelope he saw that it was divorce papers.

Cindy and Ronald had so much fun golfing and playing around just enjoying each other. "I am starving," said Cindy.

"Okay baby," said Ronald. Let's go grab a bite to eat."

"No mama cooked," said Cindy. Ronald laughed.

"That gives us a better reason to get something to eat."

"So you say my mama can't cook? That's low."

CHAPTER 16

The Next day Willie went to the bank to stop the five hundred a week transfer that was going from his account to Nikkie's account to keep her quite about their affair. Then he went next door to have a dozen flowers delivered to his wife.

Stacie stayed all-night with Christy. Both of them were up in the morning drinking coffee. "Christy," said Stacie. "Why won't you forgive your husband. I understand what he has done. He hurt you a lot but how can you carry so much hate in your heart towards your own husband?" Christy handed Stacie a letter.

"Read it please. James wrote this to me two days before his accident."

"Okay." She opened up the letter and read it to her. *"Dear Christy. You are my love, my life, my heart, and my God-sent wife. I am very sorry for what I've done to you and I know I have said sorry over and over and I have begged you too much but I won't stop till you see that I have changed. I will spend every ounce of strength I have trying to get you back. I pray day and night for you and me. There is no other woman for me. I want my wife back. You have been nothing but good and faithful to me and I've done wrong but I will fight for you. I read Psalm 23 daily. The lord is my Sheppard. I shall not want. Jesus knows what's best for us both and I will love you always and I will wait on the Lord with patience for whatever he has in store for me. I will never leave you till Jesus says it is time. Till then I will do what I have to do to get my wife back. Love you your husband, James."*

Stacie closed up the letter and gave it to Christy. A knock came at her door. "Who is it?"

"David." Christy got up to open the door.

"Come in. This is my friend Stacie. Stacie this is David. The two shook hands and said hello.

Darryl walked into the house and Cathy was packing her things. "What the hell are you doing?" He asked. "I told you nothing in this house belongs to you. Girl you come on my job with divorce papers then sneak in my house to take my things! Bitch you got nerves!" Ronald and Cindy came down the steps with some of Cathy's things.

"WHAT did you call my sister?" asked Cindy. "She was good to you. So you cheat and lie all because your wife is not up to sex as much as you so you let that one problem destroy your marriage. You walk in church like the good godly husband. Darryl you can make yourself look good on the outside to people you don't know, but God knows the real you. I personally disagree with divorce, but honey the sister in me hopes Cathy never comes back to you. Come on sis. Grab your stuff and let's go. Darryl just stood there looking at Ronald.

CHAPTER 17

Late Saturday night Willie's cell phone rang. His wife was sitting on the sofa sewing herself a new skirt. He got up and went into the kitchen and said hello in a low voice. He was hoping Joyce wouldn't come into the kitchen. "What's up baby?" said Nikkie. "Look stop calling me. I told you this before. I am back with my wife."

"Oh really?" said Nikkie. "You think? Where is my money? You are four weeks behind. Don't think I won't tell her everything. You can't just walk away like this." Willie laughed.

"Your account is closed. The money you looking for is on my wife's other finger."

"You want to play?" asked Nikkie before hanging up. Willie went back and sat in his chair and picked up the newspaper.

"Are you ok?" asked his wife. Before he could answer the home phone rang. Willie grabbed it. "Hello," he said in panic.

"Let me speak to the wife." said Nikkie.

"Wrong number," said Willie.

"I will call everyday until I get her." Joyce got up and said,

"Willie hand me the phone. Is that her?" Willie handed his wife the phone.

"Hello," said Nikkie. "I bet you want to know where your husband was on all them lonely nights you spent alone."

"No," said Joyce. "What I want to know is why do women choose men who are married. I also want to thank you because had my husband not run into a tramp such as yourself he would have never realized how good of a wife he has. Don't call my house again." Then Joyce hung up the phone.

CHAPTER 18

Sunday Morning everyone was up getting ready for church. "Where are my pearls?" asked Miss Hunter.

"Mama," said Cindy. "No one wears orange pearls but you."

"Okay ladies," said Ronald. "Is everyone about ready? Church starts in thirty minutes." Christy, Stacie, and Shell walked into church. Willie and Joyce also walked in the doors as the choir started singing. People were clapping, dancing, and praising the Lord. Church was loud and everyone could feel the presence of the Lord. After the choir it was time for testimonies and prayers. Willie stood up first.

"I want to give all glory and praise to my father Jesus who's the head of my life. I thank him for bringing me out of darkness. I thank him for my wife who stuck by me when I was out doing wrong. God is good and I can't thank him enough for my wife sitting next to me. I want to say Joyce I love you and I thank God for you. Willie sat down and people began to clap and say amen. Pastor Williams yelled out,

"Isn't Jesus good? What a mighty God we serve!" The church went crazy, the choir sang, the people were praising and crying and dancing. The sprit of the lord was there. Pastor said, "Praise him! Praise him!" As everyone began to sit down Pastor Williams asked that Christy stand and for everyone to pray for her and her husband James who has been in a coma for one month. "Keep the faith because all things will be okay when Jesus is in charge.

Darryl woke up and sat on the bed. "I think it is best you leave," said Nikkie. "I don't want to do this anymore. I can do better than this. I don't need a man like you in my life. Go home to your wife." Before Nikkie could get out of bed Darryl Grabbed her arm.

"I will kill you whore! Go to my wife? She left because of you! I lost her because of you!" Darryl got so out of control that he began to beat Nikkie like she was a man as he yelled, "You made me lose my wife!"

"Stop please!" cried Nikkie. "Stop!" But Darryl kept hitting her as she fell on the floor. Darryl kicked her and beat her till she could no longer talk. He spit on her and grabbed his things and said,

"You mean nothing to me. I am going home and I will get my wife back. She needs me and wants me. He walked out the door as Nikkie laid there in her own blood.

As church ended Willie and Joyce walked up to the pastor to thank him for everything. "It was Jesus," said the pastor. "You get out what you put in and no matter what you do keep Jesus first."

"Next Sunday me and my wife won't be here. We're taking a second honeymoon," Willie said. "I have been blessed. I almost lost my wife and I made a promise that I will treat her like Jesus told a man how to treat his wife no matter what."

"So," said the pastor. "Joyce where is he taking you?"

"To Jamaica."

Cindy, Cathy, and Ronald made it home from church along with the girl's mother. Darryl was sitting on the porch and as everyone got out the car Darryl walked up to Cathy and said,

"Please come home."

"No." said Cathy and walked towards the house. Darryl tried to follow her but Ronald grabbed his arm and said,

"Let her go man. Go home and leave her alone. She will call when she wants to talk. As everyone went into the house Darryl stood out side like he was all alone.

CHAPTER 19

Stacie, Shell, and Christy were at the hospital visiting Nikkie. "What happened to you?" Shell asked.

"Maybe this is what I needed," said Nikkie.

"Don't you ever think this is what you needed! You didn't need two black eyes, a cracked rib, busted mouth, and a broken arm." said Stacie.

"Wait a minute," Nikkie said. "All the talking all yaw did about me and married men telling me one day I will realize that messing with married men won't cause me nothing but pain. Well it caused me pain."

"You deal with married men only?" asked Christy.

"Who are you?" asked Nikkie.

"Oh," said Shell. "This is a friend of mine. Her name is Christy."

"Okay friend of mine," said Nikkie. "Yes I deal with no one but married men. I love married men and I say I am going to stop but I won't because married men go out their way to please their mistress. Nine out of ten men get bored at home and the price some of them will pay to keep the cat in the bag."

"Enough," said Stacie. "Here you are, Nikkie, lying in the hospital and Jesus can take your last breath and you sit here and talk like what you do is okay."

"Well," said Christy. "My husband gave me H.I.V because he cheated on me several times with another woman and now were getting a divorce."

"Sorry to hear that," Nikkie said.

CHAPTER 20

Willie and Joyce went to go see her mother. "Come on in you two," said Miss Murphy while she kissed and hugged them both. "I am so glad to see things working between you two. Jesus is good. All you got to do is have faith."

"Love you mom and thank you for not giving up on me," said Willie. "I promise to take care of your daughter."

"Mama," said Joyce. "We wanted to stop by before we leave. Willie is taking me to Jamaica. Our plane leaves in three hours."

"Okay," said Miss Murphy. "You two have fun and try and work on me a grandchild."

"Mama we been trying six years," said Joyce. "It won't happen." As the two went out the door Miss Murphy said, "Remember anything is possible through God." Willie whispered in her ear and said

"Mama we will work on that grandchild."

CHAPTER 21

David sat next to James Wednesday morning as he laid in the bed with no movement at all. Christy walked in. "Hi," David said. "No change yet. When he wakes up I will tell him the truth." Doctor Steven walked in and checked James temperature.

"How are you two doing?"

"How long do people stay in comas?" asked Christy.

"Well it depends. It can range from a day to years. Right now his vital signs are great and his heart rate is fine. This may sound funny but it seems like he's just taking a nap."

"A nap?" said Christy. "Well call me when he wakes up from his nap." she walked out the room and David followed. Doctor Stevens pulled up a chair and sat next to James' bed. "Mr. James," she said. "I don't know what your life was like before you got here but I pray day and night for you because your family needs you and loves you. I don't have a husband and God knows I would love one but I guess it is not time for Him to send me one yet. But I do know this, if my husband was in a coma I would never leave his side. I pray he will send me a man who believes in him." When Christy got into her car, David hopped in on the other side.

"What do you want?" she asked him.

"Look," he said. "Enough! I am tired of this. When James wakes up I will tell him everything. I love you and if we're going to be together than I feel it is time we tell him its been two years of me and you and this behind his back. I am done with that."

"Oh," said Christy. "So you're going to just hurt him like that? This may take some time."

"I lost my wife when I told her I was cheating with you and you think I'm going stay back and wait for you to tell him? You didn't wait for me to tell my wife."

"Okay I will tell him that his best friend and I are having an affair."

"Good." said David as he got out the car.

As Doctor Steven was putting her chair back she noticed a note on James' table and began to read it. *Dear James, you and I are finished. I don't want to be a part of your life. We can no longer be husband and wife. The fact that you have given me H.I.V...*

Instantly Doctor Steven dropped the letter and ran down the hallway to her office. She closed her door and started crying, "Dear Jesus this can't be true. Help him Lord please help him. Help me too Lord." She looked towards the sky. "I don't know why I have feelings for this man. I don't know him and he's been in a coma for three months. Lord here I am. Remove these thoughts of somebody else's husband because I know I need to stop. That man is married but Jesus when are you going to send me a husband? Soon I hope because I am getting old if you know what I mean."

CHAPTER 22

"All rise," said judge Lisa. "Case number 00243391ade-44632 Cathy Manns vs Darryl Manns for divorce. Please step forward. Okay miss MANNS I read over your reason for wanting a divorce. Your husband has been cheating on you for five years. He has become abusive and he doesn't go to church."

"Yes ma'm." said CATHY.

"Okay Mr. Manns do you have anything to say?"

"Yes I do. I feel me and my wife can work this out but she needs to come back home. Yes we may fuss but I don't hit my wife. I love her."

"Okay," said judge Lisa. "I order you to move back home for thirty days and I will see you two both back here to see if a divorce will be granted."

"This man is a liar!" screamed Cathy. "He his abusive."

"If he hits you call the police and we will take it from there. Case closed for thirty days." said the judge.

Shell and Stacie were at the hospital visiting Nikkie. "So when do you come home?" asked Shell.

"I don't know. I feel so weak and tired. I'm laying here looking back over my life. We was supposed to take a vacation Stacie and we never did."

"Nikkie you rest," Stacie said. "And when you come home we will take that vacation." Nikkie's eyes closed and Doctor Jeff walked in the room.

"Doc how is she doing?" asked Shell.

"Well not good. She has severe head pain and blood clots. She is going to need major surgey ASAP."

Cathy and Cindy sat in the coffee shop talking. "I can't believe this sis! The judge ordered me to go home. Where is the justice system? I am tired. Why can't my marriage be like yours?"

"No stop," said Cindy. "Your marriage got problems and so do mine but they're just different. Nothing is perfect in life but Jesus. It will be okay. Have faith. Pray on this but don't you ever think you are the only one going through and never compare your life with anyone because the outside always looks nice, but that doesn't mean it's good on the inside."

"Sis." said Cathy. "I just don't understand what went wrong. I tried to be a good wife to him and this is what I get in return. I love Darryl and I don't want things this way. I tried marriage counseling and talking with the pastor. I even gave him his alone time but what has he done? Nothing. He don't go to church. All he does is party, work, and stay out all night. Man I won't do this again."

"Every man is not the same." said Cindy. There are good men out here but some men just want more than one woman. Two women aren't anything but one big problem. Just keep your head up cause God knows what will happen next. You just got to believe in him and step back and let him work in your life."

"When are you going home with your husband? You don't need to stay down here any longer." Cathy told Cindy.

"I am going to stay as long as it takes to help my sister through this and besides, Girl when me and Ronald miss each other the sex makes me want to say I do all over again! Eyes rolling in the back of my head he leaves me breathless! So yes I will stay a little while longer. Both sisters laughed.

CHAPTER 23

Doctor Steven was talking to the head doctor, Doctor Jeff. "I need to take this test she said."

"No." said Doctor Jeff. "You can not run an aids test on anyone without their consent and you can't ask Mr. James because he is in a coma."

"I saw a note that said he has H.I.V and if he does Doctor Jeff we need to take extra precautions."

"No." said doctor Jeff. If this is the case tell your team to take extra precautions or ask his wife if you may test him. Other than that the answer is no." Then Doctor Jeff walked out the office.

Willie and Joyce were lying on the beach enjoying each other's company. I love you baby said Willie and I will do anything to show you."

"You are a good husband and I love you as well." said Joyce. "And by the way, I hope you got enough love for two more." Joyce pointed to her stomach.

"What? Are you serious? Yes! Oh thank you Jesus! We wanted one but you blessed us with two! I love you Joyce! The two began kiss and hug

CHAPTER 24

As Cathy was asleep on the couch Darryl began to rub her hair and kiss on her. "Stop." she said. Darryl tried kissing her again but she sat up. "Please don't do this."

"Come on." said Darryl. "We're supposed to work on our marriage." As Cathy tried to get up he pushed her down and said, "I want you and you will give your husband what he needs. Or do we have to repeat last time?"

"No," said Cathy as she lay down and opened her legs.

"That's a good girl." said DARRYL.

Early morning Cindy and her mother were up drinking coffee.

"I pray for your sister," said Miss Hunter. "I worry about her since she went home. I hope he don't hurt my child. What is wrong with the men and women in this world today? Cheating husbands and cheating wives and no one knows the bible I say, because if they did everyone would be afraid to cheat. What a horrible sin. All anyone is supposed to have is one wife and one husband. It pains me to see things like this. A woman is to carry herself with pride, self-control, dignity and respect. But half of them walk around letting men treat them like door mats and I never let a man wipe is muddy feet on me. I loved myself too much and Jesus loved me more."

"You are so right mama," said Cindy.

"Have you talked to Ronald Baby?"

"Yes mama."

"I just want great things for my daughters."

CHAPTER 25

Doctor Steven went to the hospital on her day off to see James. As she walked into his room tears came out her eyes. "I'm going to draw some blood okay. I promise I won't hurt you because if you have the H.I.V virus I want to start you on medications ASAP and I promise I will do what I can to help you through this. Why are you lying here so long? You need to wake up!" As she drew his blood she whispered to him, "When I get your results I will let you know." she walked out.

Cathy and Darryl went out to lunch after counseling with the pastor.

"So," said Cathy. "What you think about what he said?"

"I disagree," said Darryl. "He comes telling me I need to get to know you and your needs and we should pray together and fast on our marriage. Hell no! You need to act like a wife! I won't be in church Sunday. I am head of my house so you aren't going anywhere. But he never said the man is the head did he? I guess he didn't want you to know that."

"Baby," said Cathy. "A husband is to love his wife like Christ loved the church but you show me nothing. I love you and I want our marriage to work and yes we both should fast for our marriage. We need Jesus."

"You need him. I got cars, money, good job, sexy wife, and a nice home. I love my life and no one will change it but me," said Darryl.

Christy, Shell, and Stacie, were at the hospital visiting Nikkie. "I would like someone to bring me a pastor," said Nikkie.

"What? A pastor?" said Shell.

"I'm dying," said Nikkie. "I need to get right. If the Lord is going to take me I don't want to go to hell. It was hell here on earth for me and I want to live an everlasting life. I want to talk to Christy in private and would someone call James for me?" Shell began to cry. Doctor Jeff walked in. "Stacie may I speak to you?" he asked as the two went into the hallway. "I am very sorry but there is nothing else we can do. The beating she took caused her lots of problems. She has major problems to the head and stomach. We've done all we can. Maybe you should call her family as soon as you can."

"She has no one. No kids, no husband, and her parents passed when she was young. Please help her. It can't be her time she is only thirty-eight years old! Please," Stacie said with tears in her eyes.

"There is nothing I can do." said Doctor Jeff and walked away. Nikkie was telling Christy about her affair with James.

"I want you to know I am sorry for any pain I caused you and your husband. Will you please forgive me?"

"What?" Christy said in an angry voice. "Forgive you? All this time you laughed in my face, came to my home, slept in my home, ate at my table, but the whole time you were yelling that you loved married men I never thought my husband was on your list. I won't forgive you and I hope you go straight to hell when you close your eyes!" Christy walked out.

CHAPTER 26

David was sitting in a chair next to James. "How is it going? I see you're still just lying there. It's been four months and a lot has changed. Man I need to tell you something when you wake up. I haven't been the best friend you thought I was. Your wife and me has been together on and off for years and I am sorry for what I've done. I love her and I won't let her go. So the sooner you wake up we all can go on with our lives. As David was leaving he noticed Doctor Steven standing there at the door. "Excuse me," He said as he left.

Christy was at home on the phone with her lawyer. I want this divorce. My husband has been in a coma for four months. He is dead! This man has hurt me and I met his mistress at the hospital. I want him out my life for good."

"Look I am sorry," said her lawyer. "But till your husband signs the papers you can't do anything. So you have to wait till he comes out the coma because he is not aware of this. The judge won't give you this divorce when a spouse is in a coma. Please call me if there are any changes.

CHAPTER 27

Cathy and Darryl were at home. "Look," said Darryl. "I don't want to talk about this anymore. You knew how I was when you married me. No I've never been in church that much and yes I love women. Not you or anybody else can change me. I am who I am."

"You were not like this," said Cathy. "You changed. You act like you don't care about nothing and you believe in God. He has blessed you with so much and your power has gone to your head. But you can be broken."

"Go upstairs and wait on me to come up." Darryl said to his wife. Cathy didn't say another word she just got up and did as her husband asked because she wanted no more problems than they already had.

Doctor Stevens and Doctor Jeff were checking on James as Christy walked into the room very upset. "I want you to pull the plug right now!"

"What?" said Doctor Jeff. "You can't authorize that. Eighty percent of the time he breathes on his on. This is just extra oxygen. His heart is fine."

"I'm his wife and I decide what happens to him."

"No," said Doctor Jeff. "Not when you're trying to take a living person's life and if I feel you are a threat to this man I will have you court ordered to stay away."

"A living person?" said Christy. "Didn't you say it would surprise you if he makes it through this? He may be a vegetable or paralyzed if he wakes up and you call that a living person? He is dead!"

"I want you out now." said Doctor Jeff.

Willie's phone rang. "Hello," he said.

"This is Shell, Nikki's friend please don't hang up. She is in the hospital on her death bed." Willie hung up the phone.

"Who was that?" his wife Joyce asked as she sat on his lap.

"That was Nikkie's friend Shell."

"Oh," said Joyce. "What did she want?" Before he could answer his phone rang again and he handed it to his wife. "Hi is this Willie's wife."

"Yes. My name is Shell. I am sorry to bother you but it is my friend Nikkie's dying wish to see you both before she leaves here."

"What?" said Joyce.

"Yes my friend is dying and I am only doing what she asks me to do. Thank you for listening." Then Shell hung up. Joyce got up and went to start packing up there things.

"Wait," said Willie. "What are you doing? We're not leaving yet we got a lot more of Jamaica to see." Joyce sat down and said,

"This female is dying and the least you can do is go see her. Don't act like you didn't have feelings for this other woman. Don't act strong for me baby. If you want to cry then cry you and I got a future to look to we got twins on the way. You saying goodbye to another woman will hurt but I am strong and besides, I got you to comfort me. So please answer her dying wish." Willie stood up and hugged his wife.

"I love you," he said.

Darryl was having sex with his wife and his phone rang. He got up and said to Cathy, "Don't you move. I'm not done yet."

"Hi Darryl this is Shell. Nikkie is in the hospital dying and she wants to see you and your wife."

"What?" Darryl said in surprise. "I'm on my way!" He hung up.

"What's wrong," asked Cathy.

"My woman is in the hospital." Darryl put on his cloths and ran out the door. Cathy began to pray.

"Heavenly father I need you. I can't do this alone. I'm hurting. I try to be good to my husband but lord you see all. How much more do I have to take? I don't want to give up but I need you right now. Please help me; I'm too weak to walk away but not stupid enough to stay. Help me, and let your will be done."

CHAPTER 28

David was at Christy's house. "I don't know what to do anymore," said Christy. I love you David really I do but I want this marriage off my back. It's so hard for you and I to move forward. I understand you left your wife for me and now I want to get out of this marriage but how?"

"Look," said David. "It will be okay. All you've got to do is sign the divorce papers yourself and mail them in."

"Maybe this is wrong; you and me," said Christy.

"No this is right. People fall in love everyday with someone who is married and nothing is wrong with that," said David.

Darryl walked in Nikkie's room and Pastor Williams was praying for her. "Yea Though I walk through the valley of the shadow of death I will fear no evil. Thy rod and thy staff comfort me. For God is with you and he has forgiven you of your sins. Nikkie you are not alone. He hears you and he cares. This is the day that the Lord has made. Have faith no matter what the trouble is. Amen."

"Is she dead?" asked Darryl.

"No," said the pastor." "Prayer doesn't need to only come when one is dead. It should be apart of our daily lives."

Cindy was at her sister Cathy's house. "I can't do this too much longer," said Cathy. "My heart is in so much pain. My husband runs out the bedroom to go see about another woman. What kind of stuff is that?"

"No matter what I understand it is hard but you got to be strong," said Cindy. "See women who deals with these married men have no idea of the pain that they help cause with our family. They have no idea of what they're getting in to. See loose woman take anything and anybody at no cost to them until they find out the married man you cheating with is nothing. Some women are so dumb. If this man is cheating on his wife that means he will cheat on you as well so please don't be mad because this woman isn't getting nothing good and you're not losing anything good. Nothing good comes from cheating on your spouse."

"Mama always said there is nothing like a broken woman who is looking for someone to fix her and any man will do," said Cathy.

"And that is so true. I believe that women who date married men have lost souls." Cindy said.

"I have thought about that." Said Cathy. "I say a married man will do anything to keep a secret and the other woman thinks nothing of herself to have to sneak to be with a married man. To me I consider them to be prostitutes." Both sisters laughed.

"No," said Cindy. "How about mentally disturbed? Walking poison? Desperate lady? It would be so nice to see what a woman end ups going through after the man has no more use for her. I can only image it feels like hell."

"Do you know what I want to do?" asked Cathy. "I want a drink of nice cold liquor."

"What? You and me don't drink," said Cindy.

"I know that. So I am going in the kitchen and mix up a little something. Darryl keeps liquor in the pantry. "Both sisters went in the kitchen and Cindy sat at the island that was in the kitchen.

CHAPTER 29

Sunday morning Miss Murphy was getting ready for church and the front door opened. "Who is that?" She said as she went towards the door and noticed it was her daughter Joyce and Willie. "Oh dear Lord I didn't think you two were coming back," she said as she hugged them both. "I missed you! One week turned to almost a month. I guess you two had a great time."

"Yes we did and I made it happen. You think you just see Joyce and me but really you see four of us." Willie said as he rubbed his wife stomach.

"Yes mama," said Joyce. "You're going to be a grandmother. We're having twins!" Tears came from Miss Murphy's eyes.

"I said the Lord works in mysterious ways! You two had to get it together before he blessed you with what you wanted for years. Now he's given you two at one time! I am so happy for you both."

As praise and worship was ending with the choir's last song, the pastor was telling everyone to turn there bibles to Genesis 19: 1-38. "Okay children of Christ. I will be reading verses 23 through 26 but in your spare time read the whole chapter 19 Amen. I'm going to call this sermon 'Don't Look Back' and subtitle it, 'Keep it Moving.' In Chapter 17 Lot, his wife, and two daughters was spared by God from a City that God was going to destroy. They were told by God 'Don't look back'." Said the pastor.

"See when God tells us not to look back He means what he said. Don't look back. See most of us here today replay our lives by looking back on what could have been or what I should have done. You can't fix or change anything that is gone. The same way God destroyed this city God has destroyed our pasts. It's gone! The Lord took care of that. A lot of you right now today are still crying because a man or woman hurt you and left you. Oh well! It's gone! Some of you are in shock because someone got a better job than you. It's gone! Oh Well!" the pastor shouted. "Some of you have done wrong by everyone that crossed your path. It's gone! Oh Well! Someone here today is still upset with someone from a week ago. It's Gone! Oh Well!

"God has rescued us from a hard past. That's why we're still here because God sent us angels telling us to get up, run, don't look back, and just go forward. I will take of your cheating, lying, selfish, pain, and backbiting. Run! I will destroy this for you, but don't look back. That's where we mess up. We're always trying to look back. See Lot's wife looked back and she turned to a pillar of salt. When we look back we began to cry, wonder, regret, hurt, and think of suicide. We feel hopeless and worthless.

"I was mistreated. I was a drinker. I was in and out of prison. I was a rapist. So now you've become a pillar of salt and your past has gotten the best of you because you looked back. I want to be just like Lot because even though he knew his wife was gone he never looked back. Lot wanted what was ahead. He knew God didn't bring him that far to leave him. He didn't know God's plan but he didn't want to be destroyed with a city.

"The doors of the church are open. If anyone wants to leave that city behind and let God handle it my brothers and sisters it's not too late. I don't want to be a pillar of salt anymore. I don't want to keep looking back. Father help me look ahead to a better, bigger, and brighter day. In your name help me. Someone out there is hurting come on let go and let God." As the choir sung softly a woman walked up crying and sat in the chair. People began clapping and the pastor yelled, Praise God! Praise God! God bless you. May I have your name?"

"Marie Stevens."

"Amen," said pastor. "Are you coming by Christian experience or do you need to be baptized?"

"I Need to be baptized pastor. I am forty-three years old and I've never been baptized. I've been coming to this church for some time now and I want to get closer to the Lord. I don't want to become a pillar of salt. I need Jesus in my life."

"Amen. Praise God." Said pastor. "We will get your information and tell you when the baptizing will take place. God bless you sister."

CHAPTER 30

Darryl asked Nikkie, "Who did this to you?" She pointed to him. "No way!" he said. "I admit I hit you once but I didn't beat you this way. I was drunk but not that drunk! Nikkie I love you. I always have and my life has been stressful. You understand my marriage. My wife is running me in the ground. I have been trying to leave. She won't let me go that easy. Is there anything I can do? I am sorry." Darryl looked back and saw his wife standing in the doorway with tears in her eyes. Nikkie looked over and saw Cathy then she whispered,

"I am sorry to you for any pain I caused in your marriage. I realized lying here on my death bed that married men aren't shit." Cathy ran down the hallway and Darryl ran behind her.

Joyce, Willie, and other members were still at the church giving congratulations to miss Stevens for joining. "Look," said Joyce. "We've all been coming to the same church for a while. Lets all have an early dinner together."

"Okay," said Shell and Stacie.

"No," said Willie. "Baby we've got things to do."

"No we don't," said Joyce. "Stop lying in church lets go." Everyone laughed right in his face.

Darryl caught up with his wife and grabbed her by the arm, "Wait, listen to me," he said.

"Let me go!" Yelled Cathy. "You've done that to her! How could you?"

"Stop," said Darryl. "Don't you let anyone know what you heard in there. I made a mistake. I was hurting because you left me."

"You're a liar!" said his wife and she smacked him hard and then kneed him between his legs. As he fell to the ground she jumped all over him. "You took so much from me! You hurt me!" As she continued to hit him an officer got there and got them both off the ground.

"Miss," said the officer. "This is a hospital. You need to calm down." Darryl's mouth was bleeding and there were scratches all on his face.

"I want her arrested!" he said. "Look what she has done to me."

"Both of you are to get out of here." said the officer. As Cathy walked away Darryl said,

"Arrest her." The officer looked at the time and said,

"I would but I am off duty. You have a good day."

CHAPTER 31

Everyone sat at the restaurant eating and laughing. "So," said Joyce. "When is the baptism?"

"Pastor said he would call me with a date," answered Marie.

"I've seen you somewhere before," Stacie told Marie.

"Yes I work at the hospital where your friends James and Nikkie are."

"So you are Doctor Stevens? What a small world. So how is he?" asked Stacie.

"Fine," replied Marie. "Doctor Jeff went to check on him."

Cathy was at her mom's house telling her sister Cindy what happened at the hospital.

"It's okay," said Cindy.

"Stop!" yelled Cathy. "It's not okay that my husband beat a woman half to death. Nothing he has done is ok and I am sick and tired of you saying its ok! You are my sister and I need your help but you only say its ok when you know in your heart this wont be ok! So please stop with this crap!"

"Okay," said Cindy. "You asked for this. You are a fool because if it were me, I would have left him a long time ago. He did to you what you let him do. He had an affair six times on you and he has beat you, took money from you, lied to you, and left you when you was in the hospital having a miscarriage. You allowed him to do what he has done to you. Why did you take this? God doesn't want you to live this way Cathy. Look at yourself. Darryl wants both worlds like a lot of married men.

He wants a wife at home and a fling on the side and believe me in this world a lot of women don't care if a man is married or not. They settle for what they are and that's nothing. But you need to look at a brighter picture. You're not the one lying in the hospital. Did that girl think something good would come from this? I'm not saying what Daryl did is right but that woman thought she had something and all she had was a problem. Any woman who deals with married men is bringing nothing in their lives but a problem. I've said this before and I will say this again sis, it's going to be ok."

CHAPTER 32

DARRYL made it home. As he went in the house he was yelling for his wife but there was no answer.

Willie and Joyce made it to the hospital to see Nikkei. As the two entered her room they noticed she had been covered with a sheet from head to toe. Stacie and Shell walked in behind them. "Oh God no!" cried Stacie as she pulled the sheet off Nikki's lifeless body. "Please don't take her, please!" Willie held his head down in sadness. Joyce said, "honey I will wait outside." as tears came from Joyce's eyes. Willie walked over to Nikkie and said,

"I am sorry so sorry and when you see Jesus ask him to forgive me please." Doctor Jeff walked in the room and said,

"Stacie I've been trying to contact you. She passed about an hour ago." Willie walked into the waiting room and saw his wife crying. He held her close and said,

"Baby I'm sorry. We didn't have to come here," he said. "Let's go.

CHAPTER 33

"All rise," said Judge Lisa. "Cathy Manns vs. Darryl Manns. Will you two please step forward? Okay, we are here to see if the divorce will be granted today. Mr. Manns have you been doing what I ordered you to do?"

"Look your honor," said Darryl. "I try. My wife makes it so hard on me. She hasn't really tried to make this work."

"Miss Manns do you have anything to say?"

"I'm tired. So tired. I can't do this anymore." Tears came down Cathy's face.

"Okay," said the judge. "It's been three months and I will order a decision today. Miss Manns as of today you are here by granted the divorce. You stated you want nothing so everything will go to Mr. Manns. Case closed." As the three walked out Darryl was talking trash.

"You will be back. You need me. You don't have anything! Cindy tell your baby sister she will be back!" Two police officers walked up.

"Darryl Manns." They said."

Yes that's me. What's up?"

"Your under arrest for murder."

"What?" Shouted Darryl as handcuffs was being placed on him. "Who did I murder?"

"Nikkie. Does that name ring a bell? Let's go." said the officer.

"Cathy Baby!" said Darryl as the officers were taking him away. "I need you please don't leave me like this. I love you!" The two sisters walked away in silence hugging each other.

Joyce was helping Willie tie his tie to go to Nikki's funeral. "Please come with me." said Willie. "I don't want to go without you please."

"No you need to do this on your own. I love you, I truly do but go and show your respect. I will be here waiting on my husband so we can move forward." Willie kissed his wife and said,

"I promise I won't be long." Over at the funeral home Stacie and Shell sat on the front bench. Cindy and her mom walked in just when the soloist was singing I'll fly away. Tears were being shed by almost everyone. Marie and Christy were close to the back.

Over at the hospital a nurse went to take James' vital signs and she noticed his hands were moving so she pushed the red light on the wall. Doctor Jeff responded very quickly. "He's moving!" Yelled the nurse.

"Jesus was with him." said Doctor Jeff. "He's in shock. Close the blinds." James began yelling,

"I want my wife! I want my wife!"

"We need oxygen in here now!" yelled the doctor. "Calm down. It's okay. Your wife will be here in a minute. We need another IV bag and ice packs." said the doctor to the nurse. And get his wife on the phone!"

At the funeral Stacie was saying how she and Nikkie met when Christy's phone began to vibrate. "Hello." She whispered. "Is this Christy Jones?"

"Yes."

"I'm calling from the hospital. Your husband just woke up and he's yelling for you." said the nurse. Christy tapped Marie on her shoulder.

"James woke up."

"What?" Marie said in shock. Everyone turned and looked at her. Both of them left for the hospital.

CHAPTER 34

"Darryl Manns you've got a visitor." As he walked out to the visitor's area he saw his ex-wife sitting at the table.

"Thanks for coming," he said.

"Well I got you a lawyer and he will be coming to visit tomorrow. How you doing in here?"

"Look Cathy I am sorry for what I've done to you."

"Stop," she said. "Darryl I loved you. Why and how did this happen? You were my husband and I was your wife. Look at us. You let the Devil have his way. A pretty, single woman spoke to you with a nice smile but you should have said no. Had you done what was right we wouldn't be here."

"I will fix this," said Darryl.

"Fix it? No you can't fix this," said his ex-wife.

"No I can't but you always told me let go and let God. He can fix me. I was lost and I still am so I will wait on the Lord to fix me. You will see. I began to pray every night and I won't stop."

At the hospital James had calmed down and Doctor Jeff started asking him questions. "Do you remember your name, age, and birthday?"

"Yes." said James. "Where is my wife? I was born in Indiana. My mother passed when I was twelve and my father passed when I was sixteen. I have no children, I own my own business and I want to see my wife." Before Doctor Jeff could say anything Christy and David walked in the room.

"Hello honey," said Christy as she kissed him. "So how are you doing?"

"Fine," answered James.

"Welcome home," David told him. Doctor Stevens came in his room.

"Hello stranger. So you decided to wake up? Nice to see you."

"I love you," said James. "I missed you and I know I messed up but I will do what I can to make you happy. You are my wife and I love you."

"What?" said Christy. "No I am your wife. She is your doctor."

"Look lady sorry but I don't know you or this man." James said. Doctor Jeff said,

"You don't know your wife or your best friend."

"Sure I know my wife her name is Marie but I don't know these two."

"Baby it's me! Christy! I'm your wife. You and I was in love don't you remember? You got in a car accident after buying me flowers. We were having dinner that night."

"Okay this is enough get them out my room .I don't know these people. Get out!" yelled James.

"You two must leave," said Doctor Jeff.

"Leave? This is my husband."

"Please step outside so we can talk. Both doctors went in the hallway."

"Marie," said James. "Don't leave."

"I will be back," she said.

"Your husband may have memory loss. We will call a specialist in tomorrow to see what is going on but right now he has no memory of you two so its best you go home. At this time, he doesn't want you in the room," said Doctor Jeff.

"Go home?" said his wife. "My husband thinks Doctor Stevens is his wife and I should go home and leave him to believe that?"

"Let's go," said David. "We will come back tomorrow and maybe he will remember."

CHAPTER 35

Cindy was at Cathy's house. "So you're leaving tonight? I will miss you. Thanks sis for staying beside me all the way."

"Girl no need for a thanks," said Cindy. "You are my sister and I will always be here when you need me. You got this big house, too many cars to drive, and money in the bank. Girlfriend you set for life! Be happy and enjoy. God looked out for you and you thought you lost everything! When I come and visit I will be staying with you."

"Okay." Cathy laughed. "I ask mama to move with me and she said yes. I went to see Darryl and he is facing five to twenty years. My heart goes out to him. I loved him so much and I don't want to just leave him in there like this. I don't want him to feel alone."

"Sis," said Cindy. "It's okay to stick by him if you want. Maybe this is the time he realizes he had a damn good wife. Just because someone does us wrong it doesn't mean you should do them wrong back because as long as there is a God who sits high and looks low he will handle our battle if we put it in his hands. So if your heart is helping him through this then you do just that I got your back. I just want to see you happy and at peace .I love you."

Doctor Steven went to see James. "Hello, how are you? James sat up in his bed.

"Why are you acting like you don't know me? Was our marriage that bad? I heard you pray for me day and night I felt you kiss me on my forehead several times. You cried that the Lord would wake me up Marie so I know you love me. I don't understand why you're acting distant from me."

"James I am not your wife. Christy is. You are married to her. I wish- Nothing."

"You wish what?" said James. "I don't remember marrying her. I don't know her and when I leave this hospital I won't be going home with her. I only remember you and me so please don't try to change that." Marie got up and left.

Willie and Joyce were cooking dinner together. "Are you okay?" asked Joyce.

"Yes I am fine. I love you and I thank God for you everyday. You stuck by me when you should have left and I know it was no one but the Lord that kept you here. I messed up so much. I want to thank you for your patience and giving me the opportunity to be your husband. I am grateful to have you as my wife."

David and Christy were at her house talking. "So what are you going to do? He doesn't remember you being his wife. You were going to leave him anyway so just walk away. He will give you what you want. We don't need to tell him about us. We can just be together; you and me. That is what we talked about."

"No," said Christy. "I will not leave him to be in love with the Doctor. He is my husband and you and I can't do this anymore. As of this moment you and me never happened." David laughed.

"Just like that? You think you call the shots? I will tell him about us and about how long you've been sleeping around on him. I will tell him he wasn't the only cheater. You played a mind game with him. You didn't stop sleeping with him when you found out he had an affair you had stop sleeping with him way before that because you was sleeping with me. You were in my bed almost every night and blaming him for the broken marriage. You are a liar and if you think for one minute that you can break up my marriage and promise me it will be us and then change your mind because your husband don't remember you then you're wrong. That hurts you don't it? It hurts that he's not chasing you. Well lady this will not turn out the way you planed. So go to your husband. All dogs will have their day," then David walked out.

CHAPTER 36

Another doctor by the name of Vicki visits James and asks him lots of questions. "So you lost some of your memories and a few things you remember. This happens when someone has been in a coma for so long. James it's been six months for you but in due time it may come back slowly."

"Look Doctor I'm good. Whatever it is I don't remember maybe I shouldn't remember. All things happen for a reason. I may have been in a coma for a while and forgot a few things maybe even a few people but I still remember that there is a God so whatever has happened to me it was for a reason. I don't know but God does."

Marie was home praying to Jesus not understanding the situation she was in. "What do you want me to do?" She asked. "This is a married man and I know that means hands off. I don't wont to be a woman who sleeps or even has feelings for a man who doesn't belong to me. Help me father. Order my foot steps."

Over at the courthouse it was time for Darryl to be sentenced. Cathy sat next to her mother holding her hand. "Darryl Manns please step forward," said Judge Lisa. "You will be sent to D.O.C in Latewood Michigan for first degree murder of Nikkie. You will have a sentence of twenty years serving ten before you can go up for parole. Case closed," and the guards took him back in handcuffs to his cell. Cathy began to cry.

"Why mama? How could he have done this?"

Doctor Stevens walked into her boss's office and placed her badge on the table. "I knew you were thinking about leaving. So much is going on. James was released and he will be okay," said Doctor Jeff.

"I decided to move on. I'm not his wife and he has come here looking for me and sending flowers. Thank you for putting in my transfer and giving me a great recommendation," Doctor Steven said and then walked away.

James moved into a nice two-bedroom condo after meeting with Doctor Vikki. Christy knocked on his door. "Come in."

"Hello," she said. "How you doing? Thanks for talking to me."

"Have a seat," James said. "Start talking and I want the truth on you and me because your boyfriend David and I talked." Christy began to cry.

"I blamed you for a lot. I cheated also and I stopped loving you. Well, I thought I did. But when you went into the coma a lot changed."

"Like what."

"My feelings for my husband. I realized I need you."

"Really Christy? You needed me so much that you wanted me dead? You filed for divorce and signed my name. You also have H.I.V."

"Yes, I do," said Christy. "You and I both."

"Who did you get it from?" He asked.

"From you."

"Are you sure? Because this paper I have in my pocket said different." He pulled out the paper and handed it to her. It read he was negative.

"How?" said Christy.

"Well you stopped sleeping with me during the time you were sleeping with David. I was told that I fought for you day and night wanting you to forgive me asking you over and over to give me a chance and every time you spit in my face, not even looking your husband's way. Instead you wonted to play single and you got burned. I see we both made a mistake but I won't reverse these divorce papers. You signed my name and I see I gave you everything I had. That's fine.

You keep it all. I don't know why I was fighting for a woman like you. Please leave my place."

Christy got up and gave James a long kiss and he responded by kissing back. "You once loved me," she said and walked out the door.

Cathy went to visit Darryl. "So how are you?"

"Hanging in here. Doing pretty good. Thanks for coming. I need some more books. Will you bring me some more?"

"Sure," Cathy laughed. "You do a lot of reading."

"Yes, I got nothing but time on my hands, lots of time and a whole lot of regrets. If I could do it all over again I would. I messed up really and maybe it is too late to say this but I am sorry for all that I put you through."

CHAPTER 37

Christy went to see David and noticed that he was packing. "I'm sorry," she said. "I want to be with you and make us work. Please don't move away and leave me here alone. I need you."

"Look," said David. "Me and you will never be. You only came running back to me because your husband or ex husband no longer wants you and I don't blame him because you're a liar. You had a good husband and you decided to sleep with me. I told you before that if you didn't make up your mind you would lose on both ends and now look at you."

"Where are you going David?"

"I Decided to move back to Florida where my children live."

"So you're going to leave me just like that?" said Christy.

"Yes I am. Just like that. Don't be surprised. You left me just like that, I got a divorce just like that for you, you left your husband just like that, and so baby things happen just like that."

Sunday morning Marie got baptized. The whole church had a fellowship breakfast welcoming Marie. The choir sung, a visiting pastor preached, and all was well in the house of the Lord.

Ronald and CIndy were out at lunch. "I got to go to the bathroom. Order for us both I will be right back," said Cindy. The waitress came to the table.

"Hello handsome," she said to Ronald. "What is a fine man such as yourself doing dinning alone?"

"I'm not alone my wife is here and I would like to place my order."
As he finished placing their order the waitress wrote her number on
a piece of paper and said,

"If ever you get bored or lonely give me a call." She gave it to him
and walked away. Ronald looked at her while she walked away and he
said to himself,

"Yes it looks like I can have fun with you." Then he placed the
number in his pocket. Cindy walked out and kissed him.

"okay baby I'm back. Did you put our order in yet?"

"Yes I did," he said.

Christy was home placing a pill bottle on her nightstand and
making up her bed. She got a glass of water and sat on her bed to call
James.

"Hello," he said.

"Hello," Christy answered. "I wanted to call to see how you were
doing. It's been like five months since I've seen you and I miss you so
much. I want you back in my life."

"Christy," said James. "Me and you can never be again. I wish you
the best."

"James I can't go on like this. Please don't shut me out. Please."

"Look baby I never shut you out. You shut me out and I don't want
to keep talking about this."

"Okay," said Christy. "I won't bother you again, but for whatever
this is worth, I'm sorry." They both hung up Christy took a whole
bottle of pills, drank her water, laid on her bed, and began to pray.
"Dear Jesus please forgive me for all my sins. Life is more than I can
bear and I can't do this anymore. I am weak and my faith has fallen to
a point I want out of this world. I feel that you don't hear me Father. I
feel alone and I don't want to suffer for the rest of my life because of
what I've done." Before she could finish her prayer Christy fell asleep.

CHAPTER 38

One year later Cathy went to go see Darryl. "So how are you?" asked Cathy.

"Fine," He said. "To God be the glory. How you been doing? You still look good," he said.

"Thank you. I listened to a sermon of yours and it was great. How do you feel preaching for the lord?"

"Good," said Darryl. He has really worked in my life during the last two years in here. A lot of these men in here were lost just like me and telling them about the goodness of the Lord has changed a lot of them. I will spend half my life in here but I won't complain because this is where the Lord wanted me. I got a job in here preaching and teaching the word of the Lord and I will do it."

"This is great! Hearing you on fire for the Lord. He has changed you so much and you look good as well," said Cathy.

"I love coming to see you every week and hearing you talk like this."

James and Marie were up getting ready for church and as James was putting money in his wallet a picture of CHRISTY fell out and he just sat on the bed with his head down. "Baby," said Marie. "What's wrong?"

"I can't believe that it's been a year since Christy took her own life and I wish I could understand why but I don't," said James.

"Sometimes no one knows why things happen and a lot of us can't deal with daily life. That's why we need Jesus because we won't make it out here without him. It will be okay. Don't blame yourself, please" said Marie.

"You are a good wife to me and I promise I will always be faithful to you .I love you baby. I don't know a lot that has happened in my life but I look at this as a second chance from God. I will treat my second chance like it's my last chance."

Ronald was on the phone talking to the waitress he met at the restaurant. "So," she said. "Since your wife is working late you want to have a little fun?"

"What type of fun are you talking about," asked Ronald.

"Honey whatever you want to do because I find you very sexy."

"Well you know they say that a single woman should not mess with a married man. Someone may get hurt."

"You think? No you can only do what I let you so I can guard my heart. This is all about fun. Nothing serious. So you coming over or what?"

"Sure," said James. "Nothing serious. Just a little fun, and remember I am happily married. I will be there in thirty minutes."

Over at the church pastor told everyone to turn their bibles to Genesis 3: 13 and he read. "And the lord God said unto the woman, what this thou hast done. So I will call this sermon, 'What kind of woman are you?' There are certain types of women in the world we live in today. From medium built, skinny, tall and short. Brown eyes, or blue yes, but looks never concerned me. What I worry about is what kind of woman are you? There are many types of women in the bible and I'm going to start with Eve. Genesis 3: 13, when God asked her woman what is this thou hast done. Meaning she messed up, Eve had done something she shouldn't have done. This woman let a serpent get into their head.

"I know there are a lot of Eves out there letting serpents get into their heads. The serpents are telling them what and how they should do things. They're listening to their girlfriends telling them that they

73

wouldn't take this or that from their husband. That's why the friend doesn't have a husband. Then they say they would not take this or that from their job and telling her to quit. That's why the friend can't keep a job longer than six months. Two friends get together and talk about the other girlfriend, letting serpents get into your head. I call those kinds of women weak-minded. They sound good, look good, but what kind of woman are you and who are you listening to? Are you listening to the voice of God, or to a serpent waiting for a chance to get you caught up?

"Let's look at Miriam in Numbers 12: 1-6," said pastor. "Miriam was jealous of Moses because he had an Ethiopian wife and he had a good relationship with God. How many women are jealous in our world because someone else has something good and you don't? You want to know why God is blessing another woman. You think you do more than her because you go to church and you have a better job. You want to know why God is blessing someone that you think is so worthless. Well to God she is worthy of great things whether you like it or not!

"There's nothing worse than a jealous woman because a jealous woman seeks to destroy through family, friends, and sometimes children A jealous woman is full of lies because they are so bent out of shape that only a lie can hold them together!" yelled the pastor.

" A woman will be jealous of you even if you have nothing just because you are happy. Someone who has a nice house and drives nice cars might be miserable and jealous because you're happy with what little you have. Maybe they need a relationship with God like you, but a jealous woman will pick what part of your life they want and tell you that they wish they had what you had. Be careful when a woman tells you that because they are going to figure out how they can get what you've got by stealing it or they'll get in your way of getting something you're saving for. There's always a woman who wants what the other woman has, including her husband. What kind of woman are you?"

THE END DESREE SCOTT.ANA HAWKINS

ABOUT THE AUTHOR

Desree Scott, is born and raised in Indiana, Indianapolis. She enjoys reading, writing, and spending time with her family.